ANIMAL S.O.S.

THE HAUNTED HOUSE KITTENS

For Eva, with love – KM
For my little niece Ivy – KJ

STRIPES PUBLISHING
An imprint of Little Tiger Press
1 The Coda Centre, 189 Munster Road,
London SW6 6AW

A paperback original
First published in Great Britain in 2012

Text copyright © Kelly McKain, 2012
Illustrations copyright © Katy Jackson, 2012

ISBN: 978-1-84715-241-1

A CIP catalogue record for this book is available
from the British Library.

Printed and bound in the UK.

10 9 8 7 6 5 4 3 2 1

THE HAUNTED HOUSE
KITTENS

KELLY McKAIN
Illustrated by Katy Jackson

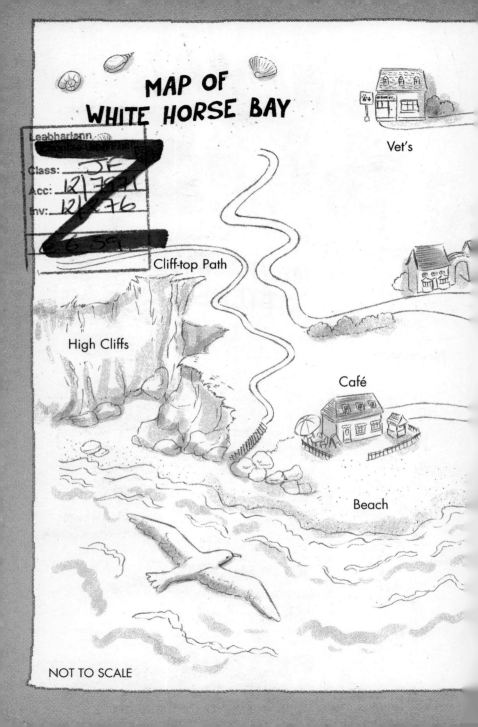

MAP OF
WHITE HORSE BAY

Vet's

Cliff-top Path

High Cliffs

Café

Beach

NOT TO SCALE

CHAPTER ONE

Amy staggered into her friend Leah's front hall, loaded up with all her sleepover stuff.

"Wow, are you staying for a week?" joked Rosie, Leah's mum, as Amy put it all down.

"Hi, Amy!" cried Leah, rushing in from the stable yard and pulling off her boots. "Gosh, what a lot of jumpers!"

Amy grinned at the pile on the floor. "Mum insisted. She says it'll be chilly in the barn overnight."

"She's right," said Rosie. "Are you sure you girls wouldn't rather sleep in the house?"

"No way!" cried Leah. "Sleeping out is much more fun. Oooh, what's in there?"

Amy took the lid off the big round tin she was clutching, to reveal a dozen cupcakes with stars sprinkled on top.

"Wow!" gasped Leah.

"They look delicious," Rosie said.

Just then, Leah's little brother, Adam, came down the stairs. "Hey, are those for me?" he asked cheekily, without even saying hello.

He marched up and tried to reach into the tin, but Leah pushed his hand away. "Get out, pig! These are for our sleepover!"

"I'll put them in the kitchen," Rosie told Amy. "Leah, don't forget you've still got chores to finish on the yard."

"I'll give you a hand," said Amy.

As they made their way across to the stables, Leah's dog, Rufus, bounded over to join them. Amy ruffled his brown shaggy fur as he jumped up at her.

"Down, boy!" said Leah firmly. Of course, Rufus took absolutely no notice. "How is your getting-a-dog campaign going?" she asked Amy.

Amy shrugged. "I've mentioned it a few times, but Mum's so busy with the builders she hardly has time to think about anything else. The B&B opens in six weeks, so she's in a mad rush to get everything finished. And once it's all perfect, she's even less likely to want a dog jumping all over things…"

"Hmm, tricky," said Leah. She grabbed the wheelbarrow that was leaning up against the side of the tack room and loaded two forks on to it. Then she and Amy went over to Nutmeg and Gracie's stables.

Amy gave Gracie a pat and stroke as she led her out and tied her up by the door, and Gracie nudged her affectionately with her muzzle. Amy had ridden the pony in her last lesson and she was already mad about her. As she and Leah mucked out the stables, Amy could almost pretend that the gentle grey mare was actually hers.

"I can't wait till we can go out on hacks together," she told Leah. "I've got the hang of rising trot now, and I hope I'll get a go at canter soon."

"You're doing really well," said Leah. "Mum says you're a natural."

Amy blushed, but couldn't help grinning. "Thanks. I've dreamed of riding all my life – it's amazing that I'm actually getting the chance to learn. Honestly, you don't know how lucky you are living at a stables!"

"Yeah, cos I get to do this all day!" Leah joked, holding up a forkful of pony poo.

Leah's dad, Dan, and her big brother, George, came out to help them finish off the evening chores. When everything was done, the girls headed back in to gather up their things for the sleepover.

"Don't forget those yummy cakes!" said Leah, as they went into the kitchen.

"How about we each have one now? We deserve it after all that mucking out!"

"Definitely," Amy agreed, pulling off the lid of the cake tin. "Hey, there are two missing!"

"Adam! I should have known he'd do something like this!" Leah cried. "Wait till I get my hands on him! No, hang on…" she said, with a cheeky grin. "I've got a better idea."

Amy giggled as Leah reached up to the spice rack on the wall and took down a jar of chilli flakes. "I like your thinking!"

Leah got out a butter knife and carefully lifted the icing on one of the cakes just enough to hide a sprinkling of chilli flakes beneath it. Then she left it temptingly on the counter.

The girls made a flask of hot chocolate and were searching the kitchen cupboards for snacks when Rosie came in and put the kettle on. "Oh, Amy, I forgot to ask," she said, as she took a mug from the drainer, "how was your Easter weekend?"

"Great, thanks," said Amy. "I spent it with Dad in London. It was lovely to have four whole days together. We went to see a new exhibition at the Tate Modern. Dad's really into art, like me."

"Well, you're in good company in White Horse Bay," said Rosie. She gestured to a print on the wall. "Samuel Trevelyan lived in this area. That picture is of White Horse Beach."

Amy had a long look at the painting. "There's my favourite spot on the sand to sit and sketch," she told them, pointing it out. "And look, Leah, isn't that the part of the cliffs where we rescued Jester, the stranded dog?"

Leah peered at the picture, too. "Oh, yeah. I've never really looked at it properly before."

"I've heard of Samuel Trevelyan," Amy said to Rosie. "Dad and I went to an exhibition of sea paintings last year. I think I saw a picture of his there."

Just then, Adam appeared, looking very pleased with himself. Leah and Amy were careful to act as if they didn't know anything about the stolen cakes. Rosie sent him to get ready for bed and they pretended not to notice as he swiped the cupcake off the counter on his way out.

Dan and George came in from the yard then and started raiding the cupboards for snacks, too.

"Hey, we bagsied the Jaffa Cakes!" Leah cried, snatching the box back from George.

"Never mind," said Dan, handing him a packet of chocolate digestives, "we'll have to make do with these."

"You only had tea two hours ago!" Rosie sighed. Then they heard a loud yell from upstairs. Leah and Amy burst into giggles. "What's going on?" asked Rosie suspiciously.

"Ask Adam!" Leah smirked. "Come on, Amy, let's go and set up camp!"

Before long, the girls were snuggled in their sleeping bags (and three jumpers each) on bales of hay in the barn. Tiger, the old farm cat, purred softly beside them. They scoffed all the cakes and biscuits as they chatted, and soon it was pitch-dark apart from the security lights shining in the yard. Dan came to check on them at about eleven o'clock, just before he and Rosie went off to bed.

"I hope you girls are going to get some sleep…" he began.

"Course we are," said Leah. "Definitely some. A few minutes' worth at least!"

Dan raised his eyebrows. "Goodnight, Amy," he said, "and you, Trouble."

The girls grinned and said goodnight.

As he headed back to the house, Leah whispered, "Do you want to hear a ghost story? I know one that'll scare your socks off."

"What, all four pairs of them?" Amy joked. Her heart was already racing, though. She wasn't great with ghost stories as it was, and out in the open, in the middle of the night…

But Leah had started, and there was no stopping her. "There's a creepy old manor house set on a hill high above White Horse Bay…" she began. Slowly, the story of the Victorian lady of Greystone Manor, who was terrible to everyone – her servants, children and even her pets – began to unfold.

"She fell down the stairs and died, but with her last breath she vowed never to allow anyone to enjoy the house again. And she's haunted it to this day," Leah breathed. "A family did move in, the Mallorys, and stayed for quite a few years, but bad luck befell them at every turn. The daughter moved to Australia to get as far away as possible from the place and the husband died a mysterious death. The wife was eventually driven out by the ghost, who passed her on the staircase every day and appeared each night by her bed to terrify her out of her wits. Now the manor is a ruin…"

Amy shuddered. "Oh, that's horrible!"

"Yeah, really terrifying!" Leah whispered, her voice full of excitement. "Wouldn't it be amazing if someone could get a photo of the ghost, and actually prove the story was true?"

Amy felt her stomach flip. "Oh no, Leah—" she began.

But Leah was off, chatting away about a ghost hunt. "Another mystery for us to investigate!" she cried. "It'll be a fantastic adventure."

"Hmm," said Amy. To her it sounded exactly the opposite.

"Your phone takes photos, doesn't it?" Leah asked eagerly.

Amy nodded. "But, Leah, I don't—"

"Then we can go straight from here tomorrow morning," Leah went on. "You've already cleared it with your mum to spend the day here, haven't you?"

Amy nodded reluctantly.

"Great. We can tell Mum we're just taking Nutmeg for a hack. I think he's got a lesson first thing, but we can set off straight after that. And you can ride my bike…"

In the end Amy agreed to go up to Greystone Manor the next day, just to get Leah off the subject of ghosts. A little later Leah dropped off to sleep, but poor Amy lay awake for ages, listening to the unfamiliar noises around them and jumping every time a gate rattled in the wind. Eventually, she pulled the sleeping bag right up over her head and finally managed to fall asleep.

CHAPTER TWO

As the yard came to life around them, the
girls stumbled out of the barn, yawning and
dragging their stuff with them. Amy was
hoping that Leah had forgotten all about
going up to Greystone Manor, but as they
headed towards the farmhouse, she said,
"All ready for Operation Ghost Hunt?"

"I suppose so," Amy muttered.

"Great," said Leah. "Now, I don't know
about you, but I'm starving!"

The girls were finishing their cereal
when Rosie came into the kitchen.

"Hi, Mum," said Leah. "I was just thinking it would be lovely to take Nutmeg out for a hack after his morning lesson. Amy could come along on my bike."

"That's fine with me," said Rosie, "so long as you're back here by one at the latest. He'll need a good rest before his four o'clock beginners' group lesson."

Leah gave Amy a sneaky wink. Operation Ghost Hunt was most definitely ON.

Amy stared up at the manor. It was a grey, misty day and the old house looked very spooky. The gates were rusty and an overgrown thorn bush wound all round them.

"I don't think we can get in," said Amy, feeling hopeful. But then Leah dismounted and managed to wrench the gate open wide enough to lead Nutmeg through. Amy had no choice but to trail along behind.

The ground was uneven, so she got off her bike and pushed it along beside her.

The garden was a thick tangle of weeds and high grass. "Wow, this place is amazing," gasped Leah, as she led Nutmeg across the pot-holed gravel driveway.

Amy couldn't help being impressed. Even with its crumbling portico and ragged roof it was still very grand.

"Imagine how amazing it would have looked in its day, and the spectacular parties and balls they'd have had here," said Amy.

"Yeah, with ladies being helped down from horse-drawn carriages by smart gentlemen, and a hallway with a sweeping staircase and a huge sparkling chandelier," said Leah. "Not that we'd have seen it," she added with a grin. "They wouldn't have let riff-raff like us in!"

"Huh! Speak for yourself!" Amy teased. The place wasn't that bad after all, she decided. She felt even better once they'd walked all the way round the manor and found every single door locked. "Oh no, we can't get in," she said, trying not to sound too pleased. "What a shame. Let's head back."

Leah frowned. "Why don't we just have a look in that outhouse now we're here?" she suggested, gesturing towards a tumbledown stone barn.

"Leah, I don't think the ghost's going to be lurking in a barn when it's got a whole house to haunt!" said Amy. She paused. "In which case, fine, let's go into the barn."

Amy rested her bike against the barn wall, as Leah found an old croquet hoop stuck into the lawn and tied Nutmeg's lead rope to it. As he got on with munching the grass, they opened the door and crept inside.

Amy shivered. "It's chillier in here than outside!" she said. Then she leaped into the air and screamed as a blurry shape shot past them out of the barn.

Leah grabbed her arm. "It's OK!" she said. "It's only a cat. Look." She pulled Amy out on to the driveway and they both watched a straggly ginger cat vanish round the side of the manor.

"Oh, thank goodness for that," gasped Amy. She took a deep breath and tried to stop shaking. "For a moment, I thought…"

"It looks like a stray," said Leah. "Maybe we should go and see if it's all right."

"I don't think it'll let you near it," said Amy.

"Maybe not, but I'll have a go," said Leah, striding after it.

"Wait! What was that noise?" hissed Amy.

Leah stopped in her tracks and they both strained to listen. A faint jumble of scratching and mewling sounds were coming from somewhere inside the barn.

"Over there!" Leah whispered. Amy clutched her arm as they picked their way through a pile of old crates stacked up by the barn door. Behind them was a rickety old table, and the noise was coming from underneath it. Leah crouched down and peered into the darkness.

"What is it?" Amy asked nervously.

"Wow, look at this!" Leah cried.

Amy crouched down, too. Five pairs of bright eyes were looking warily back at them. "Kittens!" she gasped.

"They're gorgeous!" said Leah. "All our noise must have frightened them and they've hidden."

Amy edged forward. "You can come out, it's OK," she said gently.

"Come on, we won't hurt you," Leah added.

After a little more coaxing, a couple of the kittens crept out from under the table, and the others soon followed. Amy slowly reached out her hand towards a little black one. He backed away at first, but after sniffing her fingers for a few moments, he let her stroke him gently under the chin.

"I'd guess they're about eight weeks old," said Leah, rubbing the ears of a little tortoiseshell kitten.

Amy giggled as a white one with tabby patches crept on to her lap and nuzzled into her. A ginger kitten followed and they both settled down for a cuddle. "It looks like these two are best friends," she remarked.

The last kitten, a tabby, kept mewing at them and pattering off towards the other side of the barn, and Leah had to keep picking her up and bringing her back to the others. "Oh no you don't, Dora the Explorer!"

she cried. "You come and play over here with your brother and sisters. You're too young to face the big wide world just yet!"

"Dora, cute name – it suits her!" said Amy.

"Hey, look!" Leah had spotted something in another corner. "A box filled with newspapers has been put over here for them," she said. "And there's a bowl of water, and some scraps of meat. Someone's been here this morning, or last night, at least."

For some reason, this made Amy's stomach flip. "Someone's feeding them?" she muttered, as she got to her feet. "But who? Leah, you said no one ever comes up here…" She felt more uneasy by the moment. "I think we should go. This is private property. If someone finds us here, we might get into trouble…"

"Oh, Amy, don't worry!" Leah said, as she stroked the little black kitten's ears. "We've been round the whole place and it's all locked up. You've seen for yourself there's no one here now. I suppose whoever it was must have come for a look around, like we did, and found these little ones."

"It explains why the kittens came to us so quickly," said Amy. "We're obviously not the first people they've seen."

"You know, I think that ghost story probably wasn't true," said Leah, as they played with the kittens. "I mean, it's fine here, isn't it? It doesn't even feel spooky."

"No, it doesn't," Amy agreed. "Especially not with these gorgeous kittens to cuddle! I just got myself all worked up over nothing. It's not like we were actually going to see the ghost of Greystone Manor!"

Leah giggled. "*Whoooo!*" She did an impression of a ghost coming towards Amy, who pulled a ghoulish face back.

After a while, the kittens started yawning and curling up in their cardboard box. "We'd better get going," said Leah reluctantly. "It's gone half twelve. And I don't think their mother will come back while we're here."

They gave the kittens a final cuddle and stroke. Then Leah went to fetch Nutmeg and mounted up, while Amy grabbed her bike. Leah was adjusting her twisted stirrup leather when Nutmeg gave a loud whinny and leaped backwards.

"Whoa!" she cried, as the pony skittered away from the manor. "Look!" she gasped.

Amy followed Leah's gaze, then almost fell off her bike in shock. The pale face of a stern-looking elderly woman in a high-necked dress stared out at them through a downstairs window.

"It's the ghost!" Leah cried. She nudged
Nutmeg with her heels and he didn't need
telling twice. He bolted off, with Amy
pedalling furiously after them, not wanting
to be left behind. Leah managed to slow
Nutmeg to a walk to get him through the
gate, but they did their fastest trot all the
way back to the village, with Amy right
behind them.

"I can't believe we actually saw the ghost!" gasped Leah, when they finally came to a halt outside the village newsagent's. "Shame you didn't get a photo."

"I was too shocked to think about it," Amy said. "So it wasn't a silly story after all! Thank goodness we didn't go into the actual house. Something terrible might have happened to us, like it did to that poor family who used to live there." She shuddered. "Well, at least we never have to go back to that place again."

"Never go back?" Leah repeated. "But we have to, the first chance we get. We could go after your riding lesson tomorrow. We need to make sure whoever fed those kittens keeps on looking after them."

CHAPTER THREE

The next afternoon, Mum dropped Amy off for her riding lesson. They got there half an hour early, so that Amy could give Gracie a groom and help tack her up.

"Hi!" called Leah, ambling over to Gracie's stable. "You're looking right at home there."

"Thanks!" said Amy. "I'm really getting used to all this horsey stuff now."

"You've told your mum you're staying for tea, like we planned," asked Leah, "so we can go back to Greystone Manor?"

Amy grimaced. "Yeah," she said. She didn't fancy seeing the ghost again, but she was as keen as Leah to check on the kittens.

"Nutmeg will be too tired for me to ride him after all his lessons," said Leah. "But I can take my bike and George says you can borrow his. That way we can bring Rufus along, too. He loves cats."

Rosie was striding across the yard, waving to Amy. "Oh, don't mention the kittens to Mum, will you?" Leah whispered. "She'd probably be fine with us going up to the manor, but, well, you're right about it being private property. I don't want to risk telling her in case she says we can't go."

"OK," said Amy quickly. She smiled as Rosie came up to them.

"Hi, Amy," Rosie said warmly. "All ready for your lesson?"

"Can't wait," said Amy, unbolting the stable door and leading Gracie out.

"Is it OK if I watch?" asked Leah. As Amy nodded, she added, "Maybe I'll see you have your first go at canter!"

Amy felt excited and nervous at the same time. "Maybe," she said.

"Let's see how you feel once we've warmed up," said Rosie.

Out in the manège, Amy soon got Gracie walking on nice and actively. They practised halting at the markers on the manège fence and weaving round some cones. Then she trotted a few twenty-metre circles and, with Rosie's help, managed a figure of eight, too.

"You can try a canter, if you like," called Rosie, about halfway through the lesson.

"Go for it!" cried Leah, who was leaning on the gate.

"All right, then," said Amy.

"Just get a nice rising trot going down that long side and then go sitting and ask for canter," Rosie instructed.

Amy nodded. She got Gracie into an even trot and when they reached the corner, she sat down. But when she asked for canter, Gracie's head and shoulders seemed to drop away and it felt like she was going to fall off. Amy squealed and desperately pulled on the reins to bring the pony to a stop. When she looked across at Rosie she expected to see her looking disappointed, or even cross. But she was still smiling.

"It can feel a bit rocky going into canter when you're not used to it," Rosie told her, "and Gracie tends to plunge a bit. Do you want another try?"

Amy gave Leah a nervous glance. "You can do it!" her friend called.

"Hey, who's the instructor round here?" Rosie joked.

Amy steeled herself. "OK, I'll give it a go," she said. She got Gracie back into trot. Coming into the corner she sat down,

moved her outside leg back and this time
… they were off!

"Yeah, go Amy!" Leah sang.

Cantering was amazing. Amy felt like she
was flying! As Gracie's hooves thundered
underneath her, she grinned with the thrill
of it. She was starting to feel like a real
rider now!

As Amy untacked Gracie and brushed her down after the lesson, Leah came over. "Great work on that canter!" she cried. "Are you nearly ready to go? I've got some of Tiger's cat food, just in case the kittens need it."

"I suppose," said Amy. "To be honest, I never want to go near that place again, especially not after seeing the ghost. But I agree with you – we have to make sure the kittens are OK."

Amy and Leah pedalled along the bumpy drive, not even daring to look at the manor house in case they caught another glimpse of the ghost. They leaned their bikes against the side of the stone barn and crept inside, keeping Rufus on his lead.

As soon as she spotted the kittens, Amy felt herself calm down. "Oh, hello, little ones!" she cooed, as she watched them playing around happily in their bed.

"You're all full of beans today!" said Leah. She held tight to Rufus's lead, so the kittens could give him a good sniff.

Amy picked up the white one with tabby patches for a stroke. The ginger one mewed softly and pawed at her jeans until she lifted her up, too. "These two always want to be together," she said.

"Look at the bowls. Whoever's caring for the kittens obviously came back," said Leah. One bowl was full to the brim again with water, and there were fresh scraps of meat in the other.

"Oh, sweet, look at this," said Amy, picking up a knitted mouse. It had been left by the bowls, along with a ball of wool. "They've even got toys to play with now." She threw the mouse into the air and the black kitten leaped up, batting it with his paws.

Rufus had taken a shine to the kittens, too, and as soon as Leah took him off the lead he joined in the fun, letting the tortoiseshell, ginger and tabby and white ones climb all over him. After a while, the kittens snuggled down into the shaggy fur on his belly and closed their eyes. He laid his head on Leah's legs, looking very pleased with himself. "Rufus, you old softie," she teased, ruffling his fur.

Dora, the explorer kitten, kept mewing at them and trotting over to the other side of the barn just like the day before. Once again, Leah had to keep bringing her back. She tried to sit the tabby kitten on her lap for a stroke, but Dora just wriggled away and set off again. Leah laughed. "Dora, why won't you just stay over here with your brother and sisters?" she asked.

Amy was suddenly struck with a thought. "Dora just won't stop going into that corner," she said. "Maybe she's trying to show us something."

Leah frowned. "I don't think so. There are only those old fence panels, stacked against the wall…"

But Dora was mewing intently at them, and this time when she set off across the barn Amy went after her. Dora kept stopping and turning her head. "It's OK, I'm coming!" Amy told her.

She followed Dora right to the fence panels and watched as she slipped behind them. "Oh, Dora, I can't get in there!" she cried.

She could hear Dora mewing and mewing, and scratching at something. Leah came over to have a look, too, but although the girls tried coaxing Dora out and offering her scraps of meat, she refused to come.

Leah sighed. "It looks like we're going to have to move these things."

Together they took hold of the heavy fence panels and, with a lot of effort, moved them out of the way. As they shifted the last one, they could see a watering can on its side behind it. That's what Dora had been scratching at. Now she was pacing around beside the can, mewing with all her might. Amy crouched down and peered inside.

She couldn't believe it – two frightened little eyes were staring back at her.

"Oh, Leah!" she cried. "There's another kitten. He's trapped in this watering can!" She reached inside and very carefully tucked his legs in, so they wouldn't get caught as she lifted him out through the hole.

Amy looked down at the little grey kitten in her hands. He was fragile and scrawny, and he didn't make a sound.

"Well done, Dora!" cried Leah. "You led us to him!"

"Oh, if only we'd realized what she was trying to tell us yesterday," said Amy. "The poor thing must have been stuck in there all night. Quick, let's get him some water."

Amy cradled the limp, almost lifeless, kitten in her hands and hurried back over to the others. She placed him gently on a piece of newspaper and moved the bowls right in front of him. The girls had expected him to lap up the water and wolf down some meat, but instead he just lay there and closed his eyes.

"He seems too weak to eat or drink anything," said Leah, frowning. "Oh, Amy, this isn't good. He's only a tiny scrap. It looks like he was the runt of the litter already, and now… Well, we know he's been trapped since before we came yesterday. That's more than twenty-four hours. If he won't take any food or water…"

Amy stared at her friend, with panic in her eyes. "Leah, what are you saying?"

"We have to get him to drink, at least," Leah muttered. "We need to find something he'll take some water from. A baby bottle, maybe, or a spoon."

"We're not going to find those in here,"
said Amy. She felt sick with worry. Leah
didn't have to spell it out. She could see
that the kitten was barely alive.

"Maybe we should call my cousin Kate,
too," Leah said. "She'll know what to do."

"Good idea," said Amy. "Don't worry, little
scrap. We're going to get help for you." She
cuddled the scrawny kitten close to her.

The girls hurried to the barn doors,
pulling Rufus with them, but then they
came to a sudden stop. A big black car
was turning through the gates of the
manor.

They peered out and watched as it came
bumping along the driveway and pulled up
right outside the house.

"Oh, brilliant, we can ask for help," said
Leah. "Those are probably the people
who've been feeding the kittens." She
started to stride away, but Amy dragged her

back into the barn. Something about the car made her uneasy. "Let's just stay here for a moment," she whispered. "Check out what's going on first."

"OK, but just for a minute," said Leah reluctantly, as they peeped round the doorway. "That kitten needs help."

They watched as two men got out of the car and strode over to the house. One was tall and bald and the other was squat with dark hair. The girls strained to hear what they were saying. They couldn't make out their exact words, but the men seemed to be discussing the manor. They were pointing at different parts of the building and looking at some kind of plan on a big piece of paper.

"They just seem to be checking the house or something," said Leah. "Perhaps they're thinking of buying it. They probably don't know anything about the kittens.

Let's just sneak past, grab our bikes and get away from here. We can take the kitten straight to Kate at the vet's."

Amy nodded. "OK."

Leah called Rufus to her in a whisper. For once, he came straight away and she put his lead on. Amy clutched the tiny kitten to her chest. "It's going to be all right," she told him.

The girls tiptoed out of the barn and edged along the wall. Then they grabbed their bikes and hurried up the drive, wheeling them along.

Amy glanced behind her. "Oh no, the men are coming this way," she gasped.

"We won't make it to the gates without being spotted!" hissed Leah. "If they catch us we might get into trouble for being on private property."

"Let's duck down by those bushes until they've gone," whispered Amy.

They hurried over to the large bushes right beside the manor and propped their bikes against the wall of the house. Leah held on tightly to Rufus's lead to keep him still. The men were just a few paces away from them now, and the girls could clearly hear what they were saying.

"I reckon we can carve nine flats out of this place if we cut a few square metres off each," said the dark-haired one.

"I like that idea – then we'll make even more profit," said the tall bald one.

"There's only one thing standing in our way…"

"I know," snarled Baldy, "but don't worry – if these contracts aren't signed by next Friday, we can take care of that little problem ourselves. No one is going to ruin our plans."

Amy and Leah shared a worried glance. What plans? What problem?

"Whoever they are, they're up to no good," Leah whispered.

Amy nodded. She grabbed Leah's arm and they held their breath – the men were coming even closer, trudging up the drive. If they looked their way, they'd spot the girls in a second.

"Shh, Rufus!" Leah hissed, as he started rustling in the bush, sniffing for scents. "Oh no!" she gasped, as he suddenly slipped from her grasp and bounded away, keen to say hello to the strangers. He was about to trot across the drive when Leah threw herself forward and managed to grab his collar.

There was a loud clang that made them jump. While grabbing Rufus, Leah had accidentally knocked over one of the bikes. The men fell silent. "What was that?" demanded the dark-haired one.

"It came from that bush," growled Baldy. The men started to hurry towards them.

"Run for it!" hissed Leah. They just managed to slip round the corner of the building before they were seen. They pressed themselves flat against the wall and tried not to make a sound.

"Bikes!" said one of the men gruffly.

"There must be some kids hanging around," said the other. "What if they overheard us?"

"I think we need to find these intruders and have a *friendly* word with them," snarled the first man.

Leah and Amy exchanged glances. The way he'd said it sounded the opposite of friendly.

"Yeah," said the other one. "From the state of these muddy old mountain bikes I'd say we're looking for two teenage boys. Think you can take them on?"

The first man cracked his knuckles. "Yeah, I reckon so. By the time we've finished with them they won't be saying anything about what they've heard, that's for sure."

Amy's stomach churned with fear, as she held the kitten to her chest. What on earth had they got themselves into?

CHAPTER FOUR

"No one threatens me!" hissed Leah. She looked really angry, like she was about to march out and face the men.

Amy pulled at her hand, leading her and Rufus over to the front door of the house. They hurried into the grand porch area and crouched down.

"Leah, this isn't a game," Amy said when she was sure they couldn't be heard. "We've got to keep out of sight, OK? Think about the kitten." She stroked his little head and cuddled him close. "We need to get him to eat and drink something as soon as we can."

"You're right," said Leah. "But still, if either of those meatheads comes near me, I'll set Rufus on—"

Just then, the men came striding round the corner to the front of the manor. Instinctively, Amy tried the front-door handle, but the door was still locked, as it had been the day before. "Come on!" she whispered, and they raced for the bushes at the far side of the house.

"This way!" the girls heard one of the men shout. They rounded the corner and ran into thick brambles as high as their shoulders.

"Keep going!" Leah cried, leading the way through the tangle of thorny branches. She held her arms up over her face so her jacket would take most of the scratches. Amy followed close behind, cradling the kitten in one arm.

They could hear one of the men start to shove through the brambles behind them, swearing and stumbling.

"I'm not ruining this suit," the other man shouted. "I'll go round the long way and cut them off!"

Amy, Leah and Rufus fought their way out of the tangled thorns and round the corner to the back of the house. "There's nowhere to go!" gasped Amy, as they ducked into the back porch.

She peeked out. The bald man was coming their way and the dark-haired one was clambering out of the brambles behind them. "We're cornered," she hissed.

"Run for it!" cried Leah, sprinting ahead.

Amy froze. The dark-haired man was coming her way, but her legs wouldn't move. In desperation she turned the door handle and leaned hard against the back door, hoping to force it open. To her surprise it opened easily, and she and the kitten almost fell into the house. Finding herself in the kitchen, she saw that the key was in the lock on the inside, and quickly turned it behind her. Then she crouched down, hardly daring to make a sound.

As Leah and Rufus ran back towards the
driveway, Rufus went bounding into the
bald man and knocked him to the ground.

"Oy, you! Come back here!" he shouted,
staggering to his feet.

As Leah raced away, her stomach gave a
jolt. Amy wasn't with her. Had she been
caught?

Leah hesitated. She wanted to go back,
but she knew she'd have to lose the bald
man first. She ducked into the barn, pulled
Rufus in behind her and pushed at the
rickety old door, leaving it open just a crack
so she could peer out. She wasn't sure if
the man had seen her going in or not.

Her legs nearly gave way as he got closer
and closer. She felt dizzy with relief as he
ran right past.

Leah watched him dash up the
driveway to the gates. He seemed to
think they'd run away. "Huh! As if I'd

leave Amy!" she whispered to Rufus.
"Come on, boy!"

Rufus followed her out of the barn, tail
wagging. It was all a game to him. Leah
sprinted across the drive with Rufus
bounding along beside her, then pressed
herself up against the wall of the manor
and crept along to the back of the house.
When she peeked round the corner, she
saw the dark-haired man pacing up and
down on the lawn. She ducked back out of
sight, then carefully looked out again.

Where was Amy? Where on earth had
she gone?

The dark-haired man didn't seem to
know either, luckily. He was now angrily
rattling the back-door handle. But of course
the door was locked, just as it had been the
day before.

"Maybe she ran down the lawn and got
out that way," Leah whispered to Rufus.

"Hey, you!" shouted the dark-haired man. Leah realized with a start that she'd been spotted. She and Rufus set off again, round to the front of the manor.

Inside the house, Amy's stomach lurched as the man rattled the door handle. She felt sick with panic, thinking that he might smash the glass panel above her head, and she tucked the kitten under her jacket. She breathed out as his footsteps crunched away again. Then her stomach flipped as it hit her – she may not be outside with the scary men any more, but she was inside, with the ghost.

She tried to stay calm for the kitten's sake. Carrying him carefully, she tiptoed through the kitchen and into the hall, heading towards the front of the house. From there she could look out of the windows and try to spot Leah, or see what the men were up to, at least.

The floorboards creaked as she walked down the gloomy, dusty hallway and up a few narrow steps. Further on, the hall opened out into a far wider, grander space with a sweeping staircase. It was the one the horrid lady had fallen down to her death in Leah's ghost story. Amy looked away quickly, scared that by even thinking about the ghost, she'd somehow make her appear.

She checked the front door, but there was no key. Then she pushed at a door to one side, her heart pounding. It creaked open and she found herself in a grand drawing room. She blinked in the light from the grimy sash windows. She expected to come face to face with the ghost at any moment, perhaps standing by the marble fireplace, or sitting at the piano. But the room was still and empty.

Amy steeled herself and made her way over to the windows to take a look outside.

The dark-haired man called out to the bald man, and now they were both running after Leah. Panic gripped her as they closed in. She ducked behind some overgrown bushes near the front entrance of the house, right beside a huge sash window. Out of desperation, she started trying to wrench it open, but it was stuck fast.

She glanced back. The men were only a few metres away now.

She certainly couldn't make a run for it – she wouldn't make it to another hiding place before they caught her.

A noise from behind her made Leah whirl back round. She screamed as she found herself staring at a face in the window. Then she gasped as she realized it was Amy.

But it was too late. One of the men had heard her. "Over here!" he shouted. "She's in the bushes!"

Leah wrenched at the window. "It's no good, it's stuck fast," she cried, as the men came running over.

"Keep trying," shouted Amy, putting the kitten down out of the way. "I'll pull, too."

With an almighty effort, both girls put all their strength into pulling at the window. Suddenly, it came unstuck and shot upwards. "Yes!" cried Leah.

Amy pulled her through, and Rufus
scrambled in behind her. Amy dragged the
window shut and put the catch across, just
as the men reached the bushes. Then she
bobbed down beside Leah and scooped the
kitten up off the floor.

"Wow, Amy, that was amazing!"
whispered Leah, panting for breath.
"How did you get in here?" Then her

face dropped. "Oh my gosh, I've just
realized we're inside the haunted house!"

But Amy wasn't listening. "Leah, I'm
really worried about the kitten," she told
her. "He looks weaker than ever. All that
running about hasn't done him any good.
We have to get out of here, right now."

"But those thugs are still outside," said
Leah. "They'll catch us." As they crouched
down beside the window they heard the
men talking.

"I don't understand it, that girl and her
dog have just disappeared, like the other
one!" cried the dark-haired man.

"They can't have done!" snarled the bald
one. "They must have slipped out of the
gates without us seeing."

"Look, they're only kids, girls at that,"
said the dark-haired one. "They don't even
know who we are."

"But what if they go to the police?"

growled the bald one. "They could cost us this deal…"

"They've got no idea what we're up to," the dark-haired one reasoned. "Even if they gave descriptions and we were tracked down… Well, it's our word against theirs."

"You'd better be right," warned Baldy. "Come on, let's go." And with that, they walked away from the window. Then the girls heard the car doors slam and the tyres screech on the drive.

"Well, that proves it," Leah whispered. "They're definitely up to something! I wish we'd got photos, or taped what they said. Your phone records, doesn't it?"

"Yeah," said Amy distractedly. "Right, come on, let's go."

"Why don't we look in the kitchen first?" Leah suggested. "We're bound to find something the kitten can drink from."

"Good idea," said Amy. "Follow me."

They hurried down the corridor to the kitchen. Leah took the kitten as Amy began to slide drawers open and found a teaspoon for him to drink from.

"Look, the sink tap's dripping a bit, so the water supply must be on," said Leah.

Amy hurried over to the sink and yanked at the stiff, old tap. A dribble of water ran out. She caught it on the spoon and gave it to Leah. Leah held it up to the kitten's mouth, but he still wouldn't drink.

"So, how did you get in?" Leah asked.

"The back door was unlocked," Amy said, as she searched around for a cup to put some water in.

"That's strange. It was definitely locked yesterday," said Leah. "How come those thugs didn't come in after you?"

Amy found a cracked mug on the window sill and began to clean it out. "Oh, the key was on the inside and I locked the door behind me," she muttered.

"The key was on the *inside*?" Leah repeated. "Weird."

Amy was only half listening as she passed by the huge cluttered kitchen table. She was surprised to see a half-eaten loaf of bread and a couple of apples on a wooden board, with a knife. Then as she glanced across the room she saw a pair of muddy boots by the Aga. She put her hand on the big red stove. It was warm. What

Leah had said about the key began to sink in. "Leah, it looks like someone's staying here," she whispered.

Suddenly, they heard footsteps in the back hall.

"What if it's a tramp or a squatter?" Leah hissed. "They might not like us being here." As the footsteps came closer, she grabbed a saucepan, and pulled Amy and Rufus behind the door. She raised the pan above her head and held her breath as the door opened.

CHAPTER FIVE

"What are you doing with Shadow? Who are you?" an elderly lady demanded, glaring at the girls. She was wearing a high-necked dress, and she looked extremely cross.

"Who are *you*?" Leah retorted.

"We saw you before, at the window," cried Amy. "We thought you were a ghost!"

"You shouldn't be here," the old lady said.

"Well, neither should you," Leah snapped. "You're squatting, aren't you? We could call the police, you know…"

The old lady looked surprised, then

laughed. "I'm Mrs Mallory – I *own* this place," she said.

"*You're* Mrs Mallory?" Amy gasped. "So, you weren't driven out?"

Mrs Mallory just looked at her blankly.

"Did you unlock the back door for us?" asked Leah.

"Yes, I did," said the old lady. "When I saw you out there with those awful men…"

"Who are they?" Leah asked.

Mrs Mallory just waved the question away. "Tell me why you've got Shadow," she said.

So Amy explained about the kitten getting stuck in the watering can.

"Oh, the poor little thing!" gasped Mrs Mallory. "He was there when I checked on them at ten o'clock yesterday morning. I did pop in to leave some food first thing this morning, but I haven't been well so I didn't stay long. I can't believe I didn't notice Shadow was missing…"

"You can't blame yourself," said Amy.

Mrs Mallory smiled at her. "Thanks, dear, but I do. I've been feeding them up ever since I found them," she said. "Shadow was the smallest and weakest. He was doing so well, but now, after this, who knows…"

"Who knows what?" asked Amy.

She felt Leah's hand on her arm. "If he'll survive," she told her gently.

Amy stared at Mrs Mallory. "What?" she cried. "But we found him in time. Surely he'll be fine now?"

Mrs Mallory frowned. "It's a question of wait and see," she said. "Caring for him, and hoping he improves…" Her voice cracked. It was clear how special Shadow was to her.

"But doesn't he need to go to the vet's, if he's that ill?" cried Amy in panic. "Surely there must be tablets, injections – they could put him on a drip…"

Mrs Mallory shook her head sadly. "I'm afraid there really isn't anything more we can do," she said. "The only thing that can help this little one now is care. He'll need to keep warm and I'll try to get him to eat and drink."

"Yes, I think the next twenty-four hours will be touch and go," added Leah.

Mrs Mallory suddenly looked really anxious.

"What's wrong?" asked Amy.

"I'm not sure I'll be able to do this on my own," she said. "He'll need to be cared for through the night. What if I drop off? Sometimes I can't help it, especially with this virus I've had. Oh, I couldn't bear it if he didn't pull through because of me."

"I could take him to my house," Leah offered.

"That's kind of you, dear, but no," said Mrs Mallory firmly. "He'd never cope with being moved."

Just then, Amy had an idea. "Maybe we could stay here with you tonight," she suggested. "We could all take turns to look after him."

Mrs Mallory blinked at her. "Would you?" she asked. "But you don't even know me. That really is very kind."

"Of course we will," said Leah. "We love helping animals."

"It sounds like a good solution," said Mrs

Mallory. "You'll have to check with your parents, of course."

While Mrs Mallory made a big fuss of Rufus and got him some water, Amy called home. She explained about Shadow and how she absolutely had to stay over at the manor. Mum was very surprised but she spoke to Mrs Mallory, and much to Amy's relief, she agreed. It helped that Rosie and Dan had already said Leah could stay over.

The girls watched Mrs Mallory try to give Shadow some water. After a bit of coaxing, he took a few drops from the spoon. It wasn't much, but it was a start. Then they set off to take Rufus home, have something to eat and collect their stuff.

At about half past seven, Rosie drove Leah and Amy back up to Greystone Manor in the Land Rover with all their sleepover things.

"Hi, Mrs Mallory!" called Leah, as she opened the back door.

Mrs Mallory greeted them all and introduced herself to Rosie, who was rather bewildered to find her still living at the manor. "Thank you so much for allowing the girls to stay over," Mrs Mallory said. "I'd never have been able to stay awake all night on my own. If it wasn't for them, well, I dread to think…" She ushered them all over to the Aga. There was a little box on top of it

that she'd filled with a couple of cosy blankets. Shadow was inside, lying down with his eyes closed, making little snuffling sounds and barely moving.

"Oh, my goodness. He looks so thin!" Rosie gasped. "I really do hope he pulls through!" She gave both girls a big hug, then swapped phone numbers with Mrs Mallory, and headed back to White Horse Stables.

"Shall we go and check on the other kittens?" Mrs Mallory suggested once they'd waved Rosie off. "Shadow will probably be OK for a few minutes – he's fast asleep."

"Good idea," said Leah. "I've got an extra special cuddle for one of them."

They crossed the drive by the light of Mrs Mallory's torch. Soon they were all in the stone barn, and Leah had Dora on her lap. "Who's a brave little kitty?" she cooed.

Amy stroked her, too. "You knew your brother was stuck and you never gave up trying to tell us, did you?" she said. "You're a heroine, Dora!"

Dora purred happily and rolled upside down on Leah's lap for a tummy tickle.

"Have you named all the kittens, then?" Mrs Mallory asked.

Amy blushed. "No, just Dora. Sorry, we didn't know they were yours…"

"I don't mind," Mrs Mallory insisted.

"I only named Shadow because it popped into my head once when I was stroking him. They aren't really mine, anyway. I'd been leaving scraps out for that feral ginger cat for a few months, and I couldn't believe it when I walked in here one day and saw the kittens. I thought she was just getting plumper because I was giving her some proper food! I'd have liked to bring them into the warm, but I knew she wouldn't come inside the house. And of course the kittens depended on their mother at first, so I've been caring for them as best I can in here."

"You're doing a great job," Amy told her shyly. "I love the little knitted mouse."

Mrs Mallory smiled. "Thank you, dear," she said. "It was nice to feel useful for a change."

"But Mrs Mallory, you've been vital!" Leah exclaimed. "The kittens might not have survived without you."

"Well, that's kind of you to say, dear. Look, it's silly you girls calling me Mrs Mallory. From now on, it's Celia."

Amy and Leah smiled. "OK, then," said Leah.

"It must be quite lonely up here all on your own," said Amy.

Celia shook her head. "Oh, I'm not one for people," she said. "I like my books, and my watercolours. When Gerald died ten years ago, I was in pieces. For a long time I couldn't leave the house. And then it became a habit, I suppose. I haven't been down to the village for years now, or anywhere else for that matter."

"I'd heard that you left here years ago," Leah said. "Driven out by the ghost."

"Leah!" hissed Amy, but Celia didn't seem to mind.

"Well, I don't know who added the ghost bit," said Celia, "but I must admit I started the rumour that I'd left myself. It stopped the last of the well-meaning callers. There were a few people who wouldn't give up on trying to get me to come out and do things, you see. I told a couple of them that I was moving away, and after that I hid when anyone called round. I know it sounds silly, a grown woman hiding like that, but I really did just want to be left alone. Eventually the rumour took hold and no one else came."

"But how do you manage for shopping and things?" Amy asked.

"Oh, I get by," Celia said. "You can get most things delivered nowadays."

Amy and Leah looked at each other. Whatever she said, they could tell that Celia was lonely. Talking about these things seemed to make her sad, so Amy decided it was time to try and cheer her up. "Maybe we should name the other kittens now," she suggested.

"Good idea," said Celia.

"What about Midnight for the black one, and Molly for the tortoiseshell?" Amy said. "If I ever get a dog, that's what I'd call her!"

"I like it," said Leah. She held the knitted mouse up for the ginger kitten to bat. "This one could be Poppy," she suggested.

"And her friend can be Patch," Celia added, stroking the white kitten with the cute tabby patches. "Well, goodbye for now, Dora, Molly, Midnight, Poppy and Patch," she said. "We've got to go and look after your little brother. Wish us luck."

Dora mewed and rubbed herself against Leah's legs. It was as if she really did understand what they were saying.

Amy desperately wanted to bring Dora and all the other kittens into the kitchen, too, but she knew it wasn't the right thing to do. The mother cat hadn't come anywhere near the barn while they'd been in there. As they made their way to the house, Amy saw a flash of ginger fur in the torchlight, dashing back across the drive.

"We'll do our very best for your little Shadow," she whispered to the mother cat. "I just hope it's enough."

CHAPTER SIX

Back in the kitchen, Celia made them all some hot chocolate. Leah gave Shadow a bit more water while Amy stroked him gently. "He seems more alert now he's had a little sleep," she said. "Maybe he's starting to get better already."

Leah frowned. "It's really too early to say," she told her.

"Yes, I'm afraid he's still got a long way to go," said Celia. "We'll just have to see what happens."

It was now completely dark outside, and

the big old kitchen clock on the wall said it was just past eight. When they were all settled down by the Aga with their drinks, Leah brought up the subject of the threatening men. "So, do you know who they are?" she asked.

Celia sighed. "Yes, unfortunately. They're property developers. They've made an offer for the manor, a ridiculously low amount. I don't want to sell it to them and I'm refusing to sign the contracts."

"So that explains what we heard them say," said Leah. "*You're* the problem they want to get rid of."

Amy nudged her friend. "Leah!"

Celia grimaced. "It's all right. I know what they're up to. They've threatened me before, face to face," she said. "They've told me I'll have a nasty accident if I don't sell to them."

The girls both gasped. "How awful!" cried Leah. "Why haven't you called the police?"

Celia shrugged. "I didn't want anyone to know I was still living up here. And, anyway, it would just be the developers' word against mine. I haven't got any evidence of them threatening me. Oh, I was so worried when I saw you were out there with them. That's why I unlocked the back door for you."

"Thanks!" gasped Amy. "It sounds like they're even more dangerous than we realized!"

"I'm not selling to anyone. Ever," said Mrs Mallory firmly. "I'll never leave this place."

Amy and Leah shared a glance. The kitchen was dirty, the ceiling in one corner looked like it was about to come down and they'd noticed Celia's bed in the nearby sitting room. It looked like she was only living in two rooms, while the rest of the place fell down around her.

"Are you really sure you can manage here on your own, though?" Amy asked. "I'm guessing you can't get up the stairs any more, because your bed's in there, and—"

"It's not as easy as it used to be," Celia admitted, "but I like sleeping downstairs. It makes use of the heat from the Aga, and anyway, I don't need all this space. I just like to be here, to remember the wonderful times Gerald and I had, bringing up our daughter. Carol married an Australian, and she lives over there now. They all used to come and visit – I've got three grandchildren, you know. They're grown up now, too. How time flies."

"But this place is falling down," said Leah. "What are you going to do when the roof caves in?"

Celia sighed. "I don't know. I haven't got anywhere near the kind of money it would take to restore this place properly. Even if I did, I wouldn't know where to start with getting builders and things…"

"And how are you going to get rid of those developers?" Amy asked.

Celia shook her head sadly. "I don't know, dear," she muttered. "I really don't."

Amy and Leah looked at each other. Poor Celia. It all seemed so hopeless, and there was nothing they could do to help.

"Well, I'll show you girls where you're sleeping," Celia said, as Leah stifled a yawn. "You'd better try to get some rest now, if you're going to stay up together tonight and look after Shadow. I'll be able to stay awake until about one o'clock,

I think. I don't usually go to bed until near twelve, anyway. But then you'll have to take over from me."

"That's fine," said Leah. "I'll be asleep in five minutes. I was up on the yard mucking out at six this morning!"

Celia showed them into the sitting room, just across the hall from the kitchen. Her own little bed was in the corner, and there were two huge sofas either side of a fireplace, which would do for Amy and Leah. "I'm afraid a fire's out of the question, as birds have nested in the chimney," she told them, "but hopefully, if we leave the doors open, you'll be all right with the heat from the Aga."

Amy nodded, but secretly she thought that it was even colder in the sitting room than it had been in Leah's barn.

"We'll be fine," Leah said cheerfully.

As they were laying out their sleeping

bags and finding their wash things, Amy had a closer look at the huge oil painting hanging above the fireplace. There was something familiar about it, but she couldn't think what it was. Then she suddenly realized… "This painting – it's by Samuel Trevelyan, isn't it?" she asked Celia. "I recognize the style from a print Leah has in her kitchen."

Celia smiled. "Well spotted!" she cried. "Yes, it is his work. Do you know, he used to live in this very house."

"Really? Wow!" Leah gasped. "We're in the house of a famous artist!"

"He wasn't very well known in his time," said Celia, "and he still isn't now, I don't imagine. When we moved in, some of the paintings had been left here, and we took a liking to them. Gerald and I started buying any that came on to the market. If we could afford them, of course."

"I've seen one in a gallery in London," said Amy.

"Oh, really?" said Celia. "How lovely. I used to love going to galleries."

"Maybe you could sell them and do the house up with the money," Leah suggested, "and pay for someone to help you—"

"Sell them?" gasped Celia, looking horrified. "Oh no, I couldn't possibly! When

I think of the fun Gerald and I had bidding
for new paintings, and making an archive of
all Samuel Trevelyan's papers and sketches
that we found in the house… It would be
like selling a part of Gerald's memory!
Anyway, I won't have anyone in to help me
– I can manage by myself."

Leah blushed. "I'm sorry," she said,
"I didn't mean to upset you."

"Oh, you haven't, dear," Celia insisted.
"It's a good practical suggestion. But I just
couldn't, that's all. Now, is there anything
else you need?"

"We're fine, thanks," said Amy.

"Let's just say goodnight to Shadow," said
Leah, "then I guess we'd better get our
heads down."

When Celia shook Amy awake in the
middle of the night, it took her a while to

realize what was going on, or even where she was. But then she remembered Shadow, and leaped up. "Leah," she hissed. "Come on, it's time. We're on duty."

Amy and Leah stumbled into the kitchen. They saw by the wall clock that Celia had managed to stay up until two. "He seems to be doing all right at the moment," she told them. "He's just had a bit of water, but do keep giving him some every hour or so, won't you? He still hasn't eaten, but carry on trying with that, too."

"We will, don't worry," Amy promised.

"Well, I'll try to get some sleep now," said Celia, and shuffled off to her little bed.

The girls pulled two of the wooden chairs right up beside the Aga. Leah decided that the best way to keep themselves awake was by telling stories.

"Well, OK," said Amy, "but no ghost ones!"

"Deal," said Leah, and started on a tale

about the time that Nutmeg had jumped
the manège fence with her on board and
gone haring off down the field.

After about half an hour Shadow woke
up. He looked so cute, stretching his little
paws out and giving a big yawn.

"Are you thirsty again?" asked Leah,
reaching for the water. Amy gently picked
him up out of his box and cradled him in
her arms, as Leah held the spoon to his
mouth. Then Leah put some of Tiger's cat
food on her fingers and tried to coax
Shadow to lick it off.

At first he wouldn't even sniff it. "Come on, Shadow, you have to try," Amy said, giving him a stroke. "You've got to get big and strong so you can go back to the barn, and play with Dora and the others." She tried to keep her voice steady, but the thought that he might not even see his brother and sisters again was bringing tears to her eyes and making her voice shake. "Please, Shadow," she said gently. The little kitten looked at her for a long moment, and then he began licking the food from Leah's fingers.

"Wow, well done, Amy," Leah cried. "Are you the cat whisperer or something?"

Then suddenly the lights went out.

CHAPTER SEVEN

"What's going on?" asked Amy nervously, pulling Shadow close to her.

"It's probably just a power cut," said Leah, wiping her hands on a tea cloth. "Hang on, where did Celia put that torch? Oh yes, here it is." She fumbled on the kitchen table and lit up the room with the torch beam.

"Shall I wake Celia?" asked Amy.

"There's no need," said Leah. "Our lights go out like this all the time at home. I just need to find the fuse box and flick a switch."

"Thank goodness you're here!" said Amy, shuddering. "I'd have no idea what to do."

Leah was sweeping the torchlight round the kitchen walls, searching for the fuse box. "Nothing here," she said. "I suppose it might be in the hallway…"

She padded off down the long corridor to the front of the house, leaving Amy in darkness. Amy tried not to think about walking up that same corridor the day before, with the developers prowling around outside, and the ghost… She reminded herself that there wasn't a ghost, but on her own, in the dark, she didn't feel that convinced. After a couple of minutes, though, her eyes began to adjust to the moonlight filtering in through the kitchen window and she could make everything out again.

"Amy, come here!" Leah hissed from the corridor. "Quick!"

Amy gently placed Shadow back in his

box and hurried up the hallway. "What is it?" she whispered.

"In here!" Leah called. She rushed into the front drawing room and over to the sash window they'd come through before. "Look!"

Amy didn't know what she was supposed to be looking at. "The gates," Leah whispered. "We closed them behind us, didn't we, after Mum left. Celia asked us to especially."

Now one of the gates was open.

"Maybe the wind blew it," Amy suggested.

"Not a heavy old thing like that," said Leah. "No way. Someone's here. Let's go and investigate." Before Amy could reply, Leah had slid the sash window up and was climbing out of it. Amy sighed. It didn't seem like the best idea, but she followed, anyway. She couldn't let Leah go alone if

someone was sneaking around outside.

Leah turned off her torch, and arm in arm they began to creep across the driveway, trying not to make a sound on the gravel. Then they both froze as they heard a noise by the side wall of the house. Carefully they stepped back off the drive and tucked in close to the bushes.

Amy gasped and clamped her hand over her mouth. She nudged Leah and pointed. There were the two developers, crouching down by some kind of box on the side of the house. It was open and there were wires sticking out. The girls looked at each other, realizing at once what was going on. The men had cut off Celia's electricity!

Slowly and carefully, Amy reached into her fleece pocket and pulled out her phone. Shielding the light from the screen under her hand, she set it to record. They inched as close as they dared to the men and strained to hear their conversation. Amy desperately hoped that they were close enough for the phone to pick it up, too.

"This'll teach the old bat to mess with us!" growled the bald man. "Let's see how she manages here on her own with no power!"

"Shall we do the water as well?" asked the dark-haired man.

"No. This is enough for now," muttered Baldy. "But I've got a little present to leave her." He held something up and rattled it. The girls tried not to gasp as they realized it was a box of matches. "She'll see this here and realize it's a warning. Next time, we won't just stop at cutting her electricity – everything in the barn will be up in flames!"

Amy and Leah stared at each other in horror. Amy felt sick. But she knew what she had to do. The recording was good evidence, if it had picked up what the men were saying. But she wanted to get a photo of the men at the fuse box, to be sure the police could identify them. She knew that the light would blow her and Leah's cover, but she didn't have any choice. She edged forward and held up her phone.

FLASH!

The men looked startled. Amy took two more photos before they realized what was going on.

"Hey!" one shouted.

"It's those girls again!" growled the other.

"Run!" yelled Amy.

They dashed back round to the front of the house, hearts pounding as they heard the men close behind them. "We're calling the police!" Leah shouted, as they began to scramble through the window.

Just as the men reached the window, the girls slammed it shut and pulled the catch across. Amy waved her phone at them and pretended to call 999. That did it – stumbling and swearing, they ran off towards the gates.

The girls flopped to the floor, panting and in shock. As they staggered back down the corridor, Amy popped her head round the sitting-room door. Amazingly, Celia was still asleep.

"Good thinking with the recording and the photos," gasped Leah.

Amy grinned, still trembling. "Thanks." She pressed a few buttons on her phone and they heard the menacing voice of the bald man. They listened in silence to the whole recording. "I've got it all," she gasped. "And it's really clear. I can't believe I did that!"

"My influence is rubbing off on you!" Leah cried. "Are you going to call the police?"

Amy shrugged. "Not tonight. We need to focus on Shadow for now. Anyway, those crooks will be long gone by the time they arrive. Celia can contact them in the morning and explain the whole story."

"She'll need someone to come out and fix her electricity, too," Leah added.

They made their way into the kitchen to check on Shadow. He was fast asleep, so Amy made some hot chocolate on the Aga. But when she turned round to hand Leah her mug, she found that her friend had fallen asleep in her chair!

Amy thought about waking her, but she was absolutely sure she'd stay awake herself – she was buzzing from all the drama with the developers. She pulled a tattered old rocking chair over to the Aga and settled down with her drink. Just then, Shadow woke up. She gave him a cuddle, and some more water and cat food, and tried to put him back in his box. But he dug his claws into her fleece and refused to let go, so she put him on her lap instead. He nuzzled up to her contentedly and dozed off again.

She sat there for a long time, watching him, smiling at his little snoring sounds and stroking his tiny paws. "Come on, Shadow, you can pull through, I know you can," she told him.

After a while, Shadow stirred. Amy rocked gently in the chair, singing her favourite songs under her breath and telling him about her favourite paintings while she gave him sips of water. She even ended up talking about the move to White Horse Bay and missing Dad and her old friends, and meeting Leah and

learning to ride and everything. As she stroked his head and spoke to him about what a brave, gorgeous boy he was, he nodded off. And then Amy dropped off to sleep, too.

She woke up just as the sun rose. Shadow opened his eyes and gave her another of his long, intense stares. Then he did his cute yawn and stretch, and drank so much water that Amy had to refill the bowl. She took a scrap of chicken from the little plate on the table.

"How about this? Fancy some breakfast?" she asked. The little kitten sniffed it, and she held her breath. It took him a while, but he ate nearly half the piece. "Good boy!" she cried.

"What? Where am I?" Leah stuttered, starting awake and making Amy giggle. "Oh, Amy, I'm so sorry, I must have fallen asleep. How's Shadow?" she asked.

Amy smiled. "He's going to be OK," she said. "I just know it."

And she was right. By the time Celia came in, he'd eaten another whole scrap of chicken and was looking much livelier. He'd had a little wander round the kitchen and was now purring on Leah's lap.

"Oh, I was so worried about you!" Celia told Shadow, as Leah passed him to her. She tickled him under the chin and he purred even more loudly. "But look at you now," she exclaimed. "Oh, my gorgeous boy! But why are you girls sitting here in the gloom?" she asked, flicking the light switch. "Oh, the bulb's gone," she muttered.

"Erm, it's not the bulb," said Amy.

"We've got something to tell you," said Leah.

Together they explained about the developers and the electricity. They played Celia the recording and showed her the photos. She gasped and told the girls off for not waking her and for going outside by themselves. But after that she gave them a big hug and thanked them both.

"It doesn't solve the problem of how to save the house, but it's a start," said Amy.

"It's wonderful!" exclaimed Celia. "I'll call the police right now. They should be able to get someone to fix the cables for me, too, but they might want to take fingerprints first. You'll have to give witness statements, of course."

"Oh, how exciting!" cried Leah.

"I hope I can remember everything," said Amy, frowning.

"I'm sure you will," said Celia. She put Shadow down, reached for her phone and dialled the local police station. After giving all her details and explaining the situation, she hung up. "They're on their way," she told the girls. "Do you fancy some bread and jam while we're waiting?"

A few minutes later they were all sitting round the kitchen table munching their breakfast.

"I suppose you'll need to think about finding homes for the kittens soon," said Leah.

"Yes," said Amy, spreading jam on her third slice of bread. "You can't look after seven cats!"

"They're about eight weeks old now, so they probably are just about ready to leave their mother and go to new homes," said Celia. "I suppose I'll have to contact the rescue centre in Castlereach."

"We could contact the rescue centre for you," Leah offered. "I know the people there – they're really nice."

"Thank you," said Celia. "I wish I could meet the new owners, though. It would put my mind at rest to know the kittens are going to good people, especially my little Shadow."

"They always check out potential new homes first," said Leah. "And we could keep in touch with them and give you updates…"

"Or…" Amy began. Leah and Celia both turned to look at her. She smiled. "I've just had an idea."

"Go on," said Celia.

"Well, we could invite people here to see the kittens," Amy suggested. "That way you'd get to chat to them and make sure you're happy with the new owners. We could make it into a kitten party! Everyone who's interested could come at the same time and meet the kittens, and we'd have the best chance of finding the right owners for each of them."

"Good idea!" cried Leah, beaming at Amy. "You can make some more of your yummy cupcakes for it."

"No problem, and we can make notices, too, to advertise it around the village," said Amy.

"It is a good idea," said Celia, but she was looking worried all the same. "I don't know if I can just invite people in and chat to them, though, not after all this time. And what will they think about the mess?"

Amy could see that she was starting to panic. "We'll help you tidy up before they come," she assured her.

"And we'll be on hand to welcome people," Leah added. "We could even ask my cousin Kate to come – she works at the vet's. She can give people any kitten care information they need, and make sure they understand the time and costs involved in taking on a pet. We could even make a questionnaire to help us find out whether people are suitable."

"It would be great to rehome Poppy and Patch as a pair, as they're such good friends," said Amy. "It will take an extra special owner to take on two kittens, but who knows, we might be lucky, don't you think, Celia?"

"It's worth a try," Celia agreed.

So they settled on Sunday afternoon for the kitten party. Soon after, a nice policewoman, DC Harris, arrived to take their statements. Amy needn't have worried – as it turned out, she could remember every detail. DC Harris took her phone and promised to return it as soon as she'd made copies of the recording and photos. After she'd gone, the girls made a big fuss of Shadow and went over to the barn to say goodbye to the other kittens. Then they headed up to the gates to wait for Rosie. It was time to start planning the kitten party!

CHAPTER EIGHT

"Greystone Manor? But no one lives there, surely!" cried Mrs Penhale.

It was the next morning, and Leah had just pinned one of their kitten party notices to the board at the Beach Café.

Amy and Leah looked at each other and smiled. They'd got that reaction around the village all morning wherever they'd put up their notices, and had enjoyed looking very mysterious.

As the girls waited by the counter for their smoothies and muffins, Amy found herself glancing at the table of leaflets and flyers about local attractions. There was a miniature pony farm, a steam railway, a nature reserve, old tin mines and a few stately homes. "Wow, there's so much to do round here!" she said to Leah.

"Yeah, and I've done most of it, several times!" Leah replied, rolling her eyes. She thanked Mrs Penhale as she took their drinks and muffins.

"Well, it's all new to me!" said Amy, picking up a leaflet for a stately home with a special art collection.

The girls looked around for a table, but the place was buzzing with visitors and local families. There didn't seem to be any room. "Everyone's enjoying the last day of the Easter holidays," said Leah.

"Last day for you, you mean!" Amy grinned.

"Oh yeah, you get an extra week, don't you, posh girl!" Leah teased.

"Over here, girls," called Mr Penhale, waving them to a table across the café that he'd just wiped. They hurried over and sat down, tucking straight into their muffins.

"Seriously, though, I am a bit nervous about it," said Amy.

"What, the kitten party?" asked Leah, with her mouth full.

"No! Starting my new school!" Amy cried. "It probably doesn't sound like a big deal to you because you're so confident, but ... I don't know anyone there. What if

I don't make any friends?"

"Of course you'll make loads," Leah assured her. "Just be yourself and it'll be fine."

Amy frowned. "I hope so. I'm going to miss you, though."

Leah grinned. "I'm not going anywhere," she said. "You'll still have your riding lessons on Saturdays, won't you, when you're not in London with your dad. And I'm so busy during term time on the yard after school, I might as well be weekly boarding, too."

"Thanks," said Amy. "That does make me feel better. A bit. Anyway, I'm glad we're all set for the kitten party. We've put up notices in all the shops and the village hall. We just have to pop in to Kate at the vet's, and go up to that garage on the main road if we've got time. Fancy helping me make the cakes tomorrow?"

"I'd love to, but I can't," said Leah. "Saturday's our busiest day at the stables. I've got a ton of yard jobs to do, and about fifteen ponies and horses to tack up for lessons."

"Tell me about it!" said Amy. "Mum couldn't even get a slot for my lesson tomorrow. I've got to wait until Wednesday!"

"Sorry, it's first come, first served," said Leah, with a grin. "You don't get any favours for being my mate!"

Amy grinned back. "Oh, I meant to tell you. DC Harris brought my phone back last night. She told Mum and me there's definitely enough evidence for a case against those awful men. They've had them in for questioning already. And she said Celia had her electricity back on within a couple of hours."

"That's brilliant," said Leah.

Amy looked down at the stately home

leaflet she'd picked up. "This isn't too far away," she said. "Maybe I'll be able to persuade Mum to take me there tomorrow. I know she's busy but I'd love to see their art collection, and I'm sure she'll be happy I'm not out chasing criminals!"

Leah grimaced. "Yeah, my mum and dad weren't exactly overjoyed about our little adventure, either."

"Oh, it's such a shame Celia won't go out of the house," said Amy. "This exhibition is exactly the kind of thing she'd like."

"Still, maybe the kitten party will get her in touch with people again, and she might start to think differently about going out, and letting someone in to help her," said Leah.

Amy smiled. "That's what I'm hoping," she said.

"Is that why you suggested it in the first place?" Leah asked.

Amy nodded.

"Clever you!" Leah said. "I'd never have thought of that!"

Amy blushed. Then she looked at the leaflet again. In the back of her mind pieces of an idea started to fit together. She looked at the leaflet for so long that Leah said, "Amy, are you OK?"

"Yeah," said Amy, coming back to reality. "I've just thought... These people who run this stately home, the Heritage Trust," she showed Leah the logo at the top of the leaflet. "I wonder if they'd be interested in taking on Greystone Manor and running it in a similar way."

Leah's eyes widened. "You mean, having visitors round to see the art collection?"

Amy nodded. "And the gardens. They'd be amazing with a bit of work. And the house could be restored, too. They could even have a tea room, maybe in the barn. Celia could get involved as well. Perhaps she could keep a little apartment in the house, or at least go back every day to give guided tours—"

"Whoa! Steady!" cried Leah, as if she were talking to Nutmeg. "It's a great idea. But who says they're interested in taking on another house? And even if they are, Celia

118

might hate the idea of people trooping through the place. She said she liked to keep her stuff private, remember?"

Amy frowned. "You're probably right. But then, if it saves Greystone Manor from falling down around her…"

It was Leah who had the gleam of an idea in her eyes now. "You know what we should do…" she said, with a cheeky look on her face. "There's no point talking to Celia about it until we know whether the Heritage Trust would be interested. So we need to get one of their committee or whoever it is who runs things to go round there and have a look without her knowing."

"And how are we supposed to do that?" Amy asked.

"Invite them to the kitten party!" said Leah.

"Of course!" Amy cried. But then she spotted a problem. "We can't just ring up and invite them," she pointed out. "We don't sound old enough. They won't take us seriously. We need someone who sounds grown up – eighteen at least."

"Someone who could pose as Celia's granddaughter," Leah added. "And I know the perfect person." She shoved the last of her muffin in her mouth and slurped up the end of her smoothie. "Come on, we've still got to give Kate a kitten party notice to put up in the vet's. Let's see if she wants a special mission as well!"

CHAPTER NINE

When Amy and Leah arrived at the manor on Sunday afternoon, Celia was in a bit of a flap. She was trying to clear the kitchen table and dust the dresser and sweep the floor all at the same time. "Oh, I don't think this is going to go very well," she told them. "Half the cups are chipped and I can only match a couple up with the right saucers."

"Let me help," said Amy, taking the duster from her hand.

"Don't worry, they're coming to see the

kittens, not your china," Leah added, as she took over the sweeping.

"But what am I going to say to people?" Celia cried. "I've hardly spoken to anyone for the last two years!"

"Just chat about the kittens," said Amy. "Tell them how you've fed little Shadow up, and how funny Dora is, and that Poppy and Patch are the best of friends and would love a home together. You can do it, we know you can."

"Thank you, dear," said Celia, smiling at last. "And does this blouse look all right?"

"Of course it does," said Leah. "You look lovely. Don't worry."

The girls soon got everything clean and tidy, ready for the party. Leah found a lovely old cake stand in the pantry and Amy arranged the cupcakes she'd made on it. A few minutes before the party was due to start, she and Leah went to the barn to fetch the kittens.

"You've all got the perfect new owners waiting for you, I just know you have," Leah told them, as she lifted each of them carefully into a cardboard box.

"Fingers crossed," said Amy. The kittens looked as nervous and hopeful as she felt, as if they knew what was going on, and how important today was. It was especially important for Celia too, of course, although she didn't know it. Kate had spoken to the Heritage Trust person who'd said she'd do her best to send someone over to look at the house that afternoon.

As the girls walked carefully back across the drive, carrying the box of kittens between them, the first two cars pulled up. One was Kate's ancient Fiesta, and as she got out she beamed at them.

"Hi," called Leah.

"Hi, you two," she said. She strode up

and leaned over the box. "Aw, these little ones are absolutely gorgeous! Right, let's go and find them some new homes!"

They turned and smiled at the lady and her teenage daughter who'd just got out of the other car.

"Hello!" Leah called cheerily. "If you'd like to follow us, hopefully we can find you your perfect new kitten!"

Soon, quite a few people had arrived. For the first time in years, the kitchen was buzzing with chatter, and the clinking of (mismatched) cups and saucers.

"Well, if she's nervous, she's not showing it," said Amy, nodding towards Celia, who was chatting to a friendly couple from the village.

Leah smiled. "Looks like your plan to get her meeting people again might just work!" she said.

Everyone was cooing over the kittens and filling out questionnaires. Kate, Leah and Amy sat down at one end of the kitchen table. The first people to come over to them were the mother and daughter they'd seen getting out of the car. They introduced themselves as Sue and Rebecca. "I'm very keen on the little white and tabby kitten," said Sue. "But Rebecca really likes the ginger one. Could you tell

125

us more about them? That might help us decide which one we should take home."

"Well, Poppy and Patch are both lovely, friendly kittens," said Leah. "But I'm afraid we're really hoping to home them together, because they're such good friends."

"They'd hate to be split up," Amy added.

"Mum, do you think, maybe, we could take them both?" Rebecca asked.

Sue laughed. "I'm not sure about that," she said.

"I can see on your questionnaire that you work three days a week," Kate said to Sue. "And Rebecca, you're still at school, aren't you? If you took both, they'd be company for each other while the house is empty."

"Well, that's a good point," said Sue.

As Kate went through the rest of their questionnaire with them, an older lady with grey hair and glasses approached Amy and Leah. "I'm Helen. I'm Joan Beresford's sister, she's the lady from the village store," she said. "Celia told me I should talk to you."

"Oh, hi," they said at once. "Mrs Beresford said you might come," added Leah. "Have you taken a shine to any of the kittens?"

"I really do like the black one," she told them. "Do you think I could have another cuddle?"

"Midnight? Oh, yes, of course," said Amy. She hurried over to the box, scooped up Midnight and handed him carefully to Helen. As she sat down to stroke him on her lap, he began to purr. "Yes, I think he's the right one for me," she smiled.

"In that case, you just need to fill in a questionnaire," said Leah. She caught Kate's eye and gave her a little wave. Kate came over and they introduced her to Helen.

The girls then went to speak to Celia. "I think Midnight would be the perfect companion for Helen," Celia told them. "So if Kate's happy with her questionnaire, she can take him home today."

"That's brilliant," cried Amy.

"One down, five to go," added Leah.

Celia blushed slightly. "Erm, yes," she muttered and hurried away.

"Hmm, I hope she really is OK with all these people," said Amy. "She does seem a bit flustered!"

They had even more good news when they went to talk to Kate. "Sue and Rebecca have decided to adopt Poppy and Patch!" she said.

"That's just great!" cried Leah. "Congratulations!"

"Thanks!" said Rebecca, beaming.

"You'll have lots of fun with those two," added Amy.

The girls and Celia gave Poppy and Patch an extra big cuddle and told them what a fun new life they were going to have. Kate put them into one of the cardboard carriers she'd brought along, and handed it to Sue. She took it carefully, then she and Rebecca thanked them all and headed for the door.

"Three down," said Leah, waving them off.

"We're on a winning streak!" said Amy. "Let's go and find the next kitten a perfect family!"

And they did, because a friendly couple took a shine to Molly and offered her a new home, too.

It turned out that the two young women they spoke to next weren't ready for a pet after all, though. They were sharing a flat and had thought it would be nice to have a cat, but when Leah asked who would clean out the litter tray and Amy wanted to know which of them would deal with dead mice on the kitchen floor, they soon changed their minds and left.

That was when Amy noticed a man hovering in the doorway with a briefcase and clipboard. He looked slightly confused by all the people. "He must be from the Heritage Trust," hissed Leah. "So they *have* managed to send someone. Great!"

Kate noticed, too, and kept Celia talking, while Amy and Leah went to greet him.

Unfortunately, though, he spotted Celia before the girls reached him. He strode past them to introduce himself. "I'm Charles Bannister, how do you do," he said, offering his hand. "I understand you're expecting me."

Celia looked very confused, but shook his hand anyway. "Celia Mallory," she said.

"Quick!" whispered Leah, shoving Amy back over to Celia. "Ah, yes, you called us earlier, to say you'd be coming to the kitten party," gabbled Amy.

"But I—" Charles Bannister began.

"Come over and see the kittens," said Leah, beaming. "Three have already found new homes, but there are still three lovely ones left to choose from."

Kate got Celia talking to a young couple with a little girl, but she was still glancing in their direction from time to time, so the girls had to continue with their routine.

"Do sit down," said Amy brightly. "Tea?"

"Meet one of our lovely kittens," said Leah, putting Dora on to his lap.

"Oh, I, er…" he blustered. "Ye-ouch!" he yelped, as she began to knead his trousers with her claws. He quickly detached her, handed her back to Leah and started brushing the cat hair from his smart suit.

Celia was giving them a very strange look. They needed to do something, and quickly. Just then, Amy had an idea. "What's that? You need to use the loo?" she said loudly. "No problem, we'll show you the way." And with that the girls dragged the poor man past Celia and into the hallway.

"Sorry about that misunderstanding – we thought you were here for the kittens," fibbed Leah, when she was sure Celia couldn't hear. "Celia's told us all about your visit. I'm sure you can have a long chat with her soon, when she's finished with those other people."

Amy stared at Leah. The fibs were just tripping off her tongue! "Please do take as long as you like to look around – there are paintings by Samuel Trevelyan in most of the rooms…" Leah continued.

"And some lovely architectural features,"

Amy added, remembering what Mum always said when they'd been trailing around searching for a B&B to buy.

"Fingers crossed," said Amy, as she and Leah hurried back up the hallway.

"Fingers and toes!" said Leah.

When they got back into the kitchen, they were excited to find that the couple and their young daughter were going to adopt Dora. They told the family how she was a heroine for finding Shadow, and they all gave her lots of cuddles and fuss before she left for her new home. A few minutes later they said goodbye to Midnight, too, who was leaving with Helen.

"Poor Shadow hasn't found a home," said Amy. "But five out of six is pretty good."

Celia was about to say something when Charles Bannister came and joined them. "Oh, goodness, I didn't know you were still here!" she exclaimed.

He bounded forward and shook her hand, beaming. "Celia, I'm pleased to say that we'd be delighted to consider taking on Greystone Manor. The house and gardens will be lovely when they're restored and, most important of all, your collection of Samuel Trevelyan's work is astonishing! There are forms to fill in, of course, and surveys to be done, but with a house and collection of this quality, I'd say you stand an extremely good chance…"

Celia was just staring at him. "Forgive me, but I have absolutely no idea what you're talking about," she said, looking dazed.

"Erm, I think *we* can explain," Leah admitted.

So she and Amy had to come clean and tell Celia everything. They all held their breath as they waited for her reaction.

"Well, I have to say this has come as a big surprise," Celia said at last. Then she smiled. "But I think it's a marvellous idea!"

She got even more excited when Charles Bannister explained that if the house was taken on, she could keep a small apartment within it and help with the guided tours.

Eventually he left, shaking Celia's hand again and promising to be in touch very soon.

"So, you're really not cross?" Amy asked anxiously, when he'd gone.

Celia smiled. "Of course not. I'm very grateful. Thank you so much. To help show our collection to the public, well, I'd feel like I was really honouring Gerald's memory. I do wish you hadn't gone behind my back, but…" She blushed then. "I must confess I've been a little bit sneaky myself. I've been telling people Shadow has already been reserved. You see, I've decided to keep him for myself!" She picked him up out of the box and gave him a big cuddle. "As soon as people began to turn up, I realized that there was no way I could let him go."

"Oh, that's wonderful!" cried Amy. "You can see how much he loves you."

"Six out of six – now that really is a result!" Leah exclaimed.

"I couldn't have done any of this without you two," said Celia. "Thank you so much.

You girls will still come and visit me, won't you?"

"Of course we will," Amy promised. "We'll be desperate to know how Shadow's getting on. And to find out what happens with the Heritage Trust, of course."

Celia smiled. "Thank you again. This is all down to you, you know!"

Leah and Amy beamed at each other. They'd found homes for all the kittens, and now it looked like they'd found a way for Celia and Shadow to stay in their home, too!

"Are you sure you girls don't want a lift back down to the village?" asked Kate, as she was getting ready to go.

"Thanks, but we've got our bikes," said Leah.

They all said goodbye and headed out of the back door. "Good luck, we hope it all works out," called Amy, as they set off down the drive.

Celia smiled at them and made Shadow wave goodbye with a little grey paw. "Thanks again for everything!" she called.

"Well, that's the end of another Animal S.O.S. adventure," said Leah, as she and Amy picked up their bikes.

Amy smiled. "I wonder what our next mission will be?"

ANIMAL S.O.S.

THE MYSTERY OF THE CLIFF-TOP DOG

OUT NOW!

KELLY McKAIN

THE MYSTERY OF THE CLIFF-TOP DOG

When Amy moves to White Horse Bay she can't wait to start her riding lessons at the local stables. There she meets fiery Leah, and soon the girls are caught up in their first adventure. Amy has spotted an injured dog stranded on a cliff and the owners are nowhere to be seen. With a terrible storm coming the girls need a plan, and fast…

Look out for Amy and Leah's next
adventure, coming soon!

ANIMAL
S.O.S.

To find out more about Kelly McKain,
visit her website:

www.kellymckain.co.uk